An I Can Read Book™

ELVIS the Rooster
And the Magic Words

Den s
Cazet

R
JE

HarperCollins*Publishers*

For Steve, king of the roost,
and Yvonne, his queen

HarperCollins®, 🅲®, and I Can Read Book® are trademarks of HarperCollins Publishers Inc.

Library of Congress Cataloging-in-Publication Data
Cazet, Denys.
  Elvis the rooster and the magic words / Denys Cazet. —1st ed.
    p.   cm. — (An I can read book)
  Summary: Elvis, a proud rooster, learns a lesson in manners after a handsome peacock visits his farm.
    ISBN 0-06-000509-2 — ISBN 0-06-000510-6 (lib. bdg.) — ISBN 0-06-000511-4 (pbk.)
    [1. Roosters—Fiction. 2. Peacocks—Fiction. 3. Etiquette—Fiction.] I. Title. II. Series.
PZ7.C2985En 2004   2003008334
[E]—dc21

❖

Sunrise

The sun rose behind the old oak tree
on the hill.

Elvis stopped crowing.

"Another perfect sunrise,"

he muttered. "Am I good, or what?"

Elvis fluttered down from the barn

and strutted across the barnyard.

Pollo, a rooster from the farm

next door, was waiting.

"Thanks for asking me to breakfast,"

said Pollo.

"Yeah, yeah," said Elvis.

"Where's Little Willie?"

"He'll be late," said Pollo.

"He's hiring someone

to do his crowing for him."

"What?" shouted Elvis.

"Who ever heard of such a thing?"

Pollo shrugged.

"Things change," he said.

"Not on my farm!" said Elvis.

"On my farm, I do the crowing.

On my farm, I'm the boss.

On my farm, nothing changes!"

Can a Cow Bring Up the Sun?

Elvis and Pollo sat down at the table.

"Juice," said Elvis.

A chicken named Gina poured juice.

"Roosters crow!" said Elvis.

"You don't hire someone to do it!"

"Little Willie is busy," said Pollo.

"He has a feather in every pie."

9

"It's against nature!" said Elvis.

"Roosters crow. Cows moo.

Can a cow bring up the sun?"

Gina poured more juice.

"Thank you," said Pollo.

"HA!" said Elvis. "See what I mean?"

"What?" said Pollo.

"All I said was 'thank you.'"

"That's how it starts," said Elvis.

"Next, you hire out your crowing.

You forget to brag.

You lose your strut.

You're not the boss anymore.

You're not even a rooster anymore!"

Little Willie

A huge goose filled the doorway.

He wore dark glasses

and a toothpick hung from his beak.

"Okay, boss," he said.

Little Willie slipped into the room.

"Good morning," he said.

The chickens served breakfast.

"Thank you," said Pollo.

"Thank you," said Little Willie.

"About time," said Elvis.

When Elvis was finished,

he pushed his plate away.

"Back rub!" he said.

Gina and another chicken

named Lia rushed over.

"See?" said Elvis. "In this coop,

a rooster is still a rooster."

The goose took out his toothpick.

He leaned over Elvis.

"Are you saying

Little Willie is NOT a rooster?"

"Uh . . . no," said Elvis. "I just meant—"

Little Willie raised his wing.

The goose stepped back.

"Elvis," said Little Willie softly.

"Would you do me a favor . . . please?"

Elvis shrugged. "Sure," he said.

"A friend of mine is coming to town,"

said Little Willie.

"May he stay here for a few days?"

"What's his name?" Elvis asked.

"Cluck," said Little Willie.

"Cluck Gable."

Cluck Gable

Elvis strutted across the barnyard.

"Another perfect sunrise," he said.

He went into the hen house

and looked at the table.

It was empty.

"Hey!" he said.

"Where's my breakfast?"

The chickens stood in a circle

around a large green bird.

"Who are you?" asked Elvis.

The green bird handed Elvis a card.

Cluck Gable

Good-looking Peacock

Little Willie, Inc.

"Call me Cluck," said the peacock.

"Listen, Chuck," said Elvis.

"Around here, I'm the boss and—"

Elvis stopped.

He looked at the peacock's feet.

"Those are my slippers!" he said.

"I know," said Cluck.

"The chickens gave them to me

after they fixed your bed for me."

"My bed?" said Elvis.

The peacock nodded.

"Where am I supposed to sleep?"

asked Elvis.

Cluck pointed at the floor.

"What about my breakfast?"

asked Elvis.

"I ate it," said Cluck.

Elvis puffed up his chest.

"Listen," said Elvis, "Little Willie

may be a friend of yours,

but around here, I'm still the—"

Suddenly, the peacock
snapped open his tail feathers.

Rainbows flashed in the light.

The chickens swooned.

Elvis didn't feel so good himself.

Magic Words

The next morning,

Elvis dragged himself off the roof.

"I feel like a pretzel," he muttered.

He limped into the hen house.

The chickens were watching Cluck

do magic tricks.

They giggled.

Elvis rolled his eyes.

"Breakfast," he said.

"Just a minute," said Lia.

The chickens watched more magic.

"Hey!" said Elvis. "Breakfast!"

"Just a minute," said Gina.

The peacock did a card trick.

"Hey," said Elvis.

"What do I have to do?

Send up a flare?"

31

Cluck put his arm around Elvis.

"Maybe you should try

the magic words," he said.

"Hocus pocus?" Elvis asked.

"*Please* and *thank you*," said Cluck.

Breakfast

The sun rose slowly

in the gray morning sky.

"Magic words!" Elvis wheezed. "HA!"

He staggered down the ladder.

"Pleases and thank-yous. HA!"

Elvis teetered across the barnyard.

"I'll show Mr. La-di-da who's boss!"

Elvis combed his comb.

He put on his best smile

and went into the hen house.

"Breakfast!" he said cheerfully.

"On the table,"

said a chicken named Daniela.

Elvis looked at his breakfast.

Three kernels of dry corn

lay on a rusty tin plate.

Elvis looked at Cluck.

"You and your magic words!

I'm a rooster and roosters never—"

Suddenly, the peacock

snapped open his tail feathers.

The chickens swooned, again.

"Don't do that!" Elvis shouted.

"PLEASE!"

The Note

A cold rain fell from the dark sky.

Elvis stumbled in the mud.

He pulled himself up onto one knee

and looked up into the gloom.

It began to hail.

It hailed harder and harder.

"Suffering stinkweed!" he yelled.

Elvis crawled onto the coop porch.

"I give up," he gasped. "I—"

Elvis stopped.

He saw a note nailed to the door.

Dear Elvis,

Thanks for the use of the coop.

I would have stayed longer

but Little Willie called.

Again, thank you.

Cluck Gable

"HA!" cried Elvis.

"So much for Mr. Fancy Pants!"

Elvis marched into the hen house.

"Breakfast!" he demanded.

Gina and Lia each carried a plate

to the table.

Elvis's favorite breakfast was on one.

On the other was some dried corn.

"Well?" said Daniela.

"Well what?" said Elvis.

"What do you say?" asked Daniela.

"Gimme," said Elvis.

Daniela nodded, and Gina

set down the plate of dried corn.

Those Words Again

Elvis stared at the dry corn.

He looked at the chickens.

The chickens looked at Elvis.

Elvis sighed.

He got up from the table

and looked into the barnyard.

He didn't see any other roosters.

He pulled down the shade.

He took a deep breath.

"Okay," he said. "Please!"

The chickens gave Elvis

his favorite breakfast.

Lia brought him his slippers.

Gina helped him put on his robe.

Daniela waited.

"What?" said Elvis.

"The magic words," said Daniela.

"Hocus pocus?" said Elvis.

"No," said Daniela. "*Please* AND . . ."

". . . and?" said Elvis.

". . . and *thank you*," said Daniela.

"Oh, right," said Elvis.

"You're welcome."